SUPERMAN™

AN ORIGIN STORY

Curious
Fox

Published in the United Kingdom in 2016 by Curious Fox
an imprint of Capstone Global Library Limited,
264 Banbury Road, Oxford, OX2 7DY
Registered company number: 6695582
www.curious-fox.com

First published by Stone Arch Books
a Capstone imprint
1710 Roe Crest Drive
North Mankato, MN 56003
www.mycapstone.com

STAR35962

ISBN 978 1 78202 481 1
19 18 17 16 15
10 9 8 7 6 5 4 3 2 1

A full catalogue record for this book is available from the British Library

Contributing artists: Tim Levins, Dan Schoening, Erik Doescher,
Mike DeCarlo, Lee Loughridge and Ethen Beavers
Designed by Hilary Wacholz

Printed and bound in China

SUPERMAN™

AN ORIGIN STORY

WRITTEN BY
MATTHEW K. MANNING

ILLUSTRATED BY
LUCIANO VECCHIO

SUPERMAN CREATED BY
JERRY SIEGEL AND JOE SHUSTER
BY SPECIAL ARRANGEMENT WITH
THE JERRY SIEGEL FAMILY

They say the universe began
with a big bang.

The same can be said for
the life of the boy who would
become known as Superman.

In a distant part of the universe, the planet Krypton is destroyed. A lone rocket ship survives the explosion.

On board this tiny spacecraft is a single passenger. A little baby called Kal-El.

Kal-El holds tight to the blanket his mother gave him. He dreams of being held in her arms.

When the rocket ship lands, the baby wakes up.

Cold air fills his lungs. He opens his eyes. Two friendly faces are looking back at him.

"We're keeping him, Jonathan," says the woman. Kal-El likes her face. Her smile is warm. It is just like his mother's smile.

"Oh, Martha," says the man next to her. "We don't know anything about this child. We can't just take him."

Kal-El reaches out. He wraps his hand around the man's finger.

Now Jonathan is smiling, too.

"What do you think of the name Clark?" asks the woman.

With his eyes open wide, Kal-El smiles at the woman.

Sixteen years later, Kal-El is still smiling.

His friends call him Clark now. He leads a normal life in the town of Smallville, Kansas. Or at least he did until one fateful day.

Lana Lang tries to recite this week's poem from memory in front of the class. At the same time, Clark wonders what he'll be having for lunch.

Suddenly, he realizes that he's looking right through the wall into the school canteen.

"I think I've lost my keys," says Mrs Owens.

Mrs Lancaster sighs. "Again, Gladys?" she asks. "I'll help you look for them."

Clark is seeing into the canteen. He can hear the cooks' conversation. It's like they are in the room with him!

"Are you okay, Clark?" asks Mrs Brown.

Clark nods his head. But he doesn't really feel okay.

Later, the old barn door slowly creaks open.

Jonathan and Martha Kent glance at each other. Then they walk inside.

Clark's parents have been worried ever since Clark got home from school that day. He has told them what happened at school. He has lots of questions for them.

Now, Clark will get some answers.

Jonathan lifts up the dusty lid of a wooden box. Clark has never paid much attention to the box before today.

Inside is a small metal rocket ship. It looks familiar to Clark. But he doesn't know why.

"This is what we found you in," says Jonathan.

Clark doesn't know what to think.

Then his father hands Clark a small box. It is the only thing they found inside the ship with Clark all those years ago.

Jonathan and Martha never knew

what the box was for. But in Clark's

hands, the device lights up.

Something that looks like an "S"

fills the screen.

Light from the device shines on Clark's forehead.

The world falls away around Clark. He no longer sees Smallville.

Instead, he sees the planet Krypton around him.

Clark watches as a man called Jor-El hands a baby to his wife, Lara.

Lara is crying. She is hugging the child tightly.

Beneath their feet, the ground begins to shake. They both know they must say goodbye to their son.

If baby Kal-El is to survive, he must leave Krypton. Jor-El and Lara place him in a rocket ship.

The ship takes off just as the world around it explodes.

Clark opens his eyes. Smallville is back.

Jonathan and Martha Kent watch as Clark comes back into focus.

Clark looks at them. Then he runs out of the barn. And he keeps on running.

Clark doesn't notice that he is moving faster than normal.

Soon he is dashing through the fields with super-speed!

He doesn't even notice when his feet lift off the ground.

He doesn't notice that he's flying until it's already happening.

A short while later, Clark has flown back to the family barn.

Clark lands on the ground.

For a long moment, he and his parents just stare at each other.

Then Clark hugs them. Now he knows who he is. He knows where he came from. And he knows what he has to do on planet Earth.

Years later, Clark is travelling on a train. His eyes are closed when he hears the conductor.

"Last stop!" the man shouts. "Metropolis! Everybody off!"

Clark adjusts his hat as he steps off the train. He looks around at his new home.

Clark left Smallville to come to Metropolis.

The giant city is very different from his small hometown. It is unlike any other place he has visited before. But Clark cannot go sightseeing just yet.

Today is Clark's first day at his new job. He is now a reporter for a famous newspaper called the *Daily Planet.*

Everyone is so busy at the *Daily Planet* that they hardly notice Clark.

Clark's boss, Perry White, is too busy to give Clark his first assignment.

Instead, Perry introduces him to his new partner, Lois Lane.

Before he knows it, Clark's trying his best to keep up with Lois.

Together, they go to cover a press conference held by billionaire Lex Luthor. He reveals his new robot.

Clark knows all about Lex Luthor. Long before he moved to Metropolis, Clark had studied Lex's life.

The people of Metropolis think Luthor is a hero. But Clark knows better.

Lex is evil. He will do anything to make money.

Suddenly Lex's giant robot starts to malfunction.

Luthor always tries to save money by cutting costs, so Clark isn't at all surprised.

The people in the crowd are too scared and busy to notice that Clark changes outfits.

The robot tries to attack a
red-headed young man. But
Clark saves him.

This is the moment Clark has prepared for all his life.

He has been sent to Earth to protect others.

Earth's yellow Sun gives Clark's alien body extra energy.

He gains the powers of super-strength, super-speed and invulnerability.

A metal robot doesn't stand a chance against the Man of Steel.

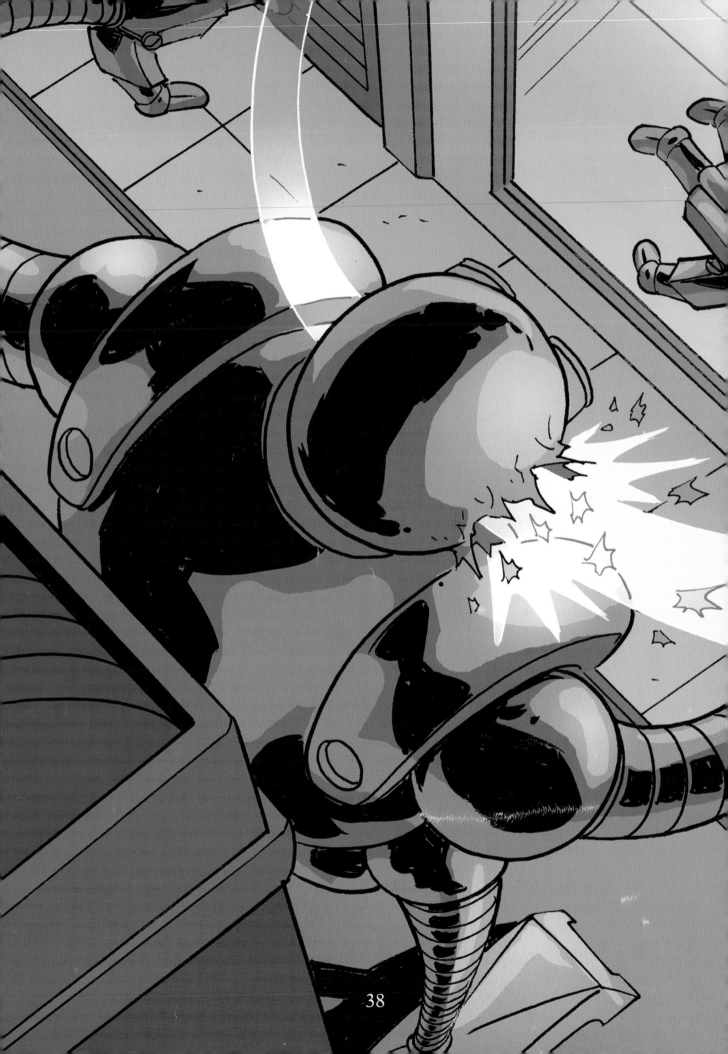

The red-headed young
man snaps a photo of
Superman in action.

"Superman!" Lois Lane cries out. She is amazed by this new hero of Metropolis.

Clark smiles. Then he soars into the air.

He likes Lois very much. And he likes the name Superman, too.

Look, up in the sky!

Is it a bird?

Is it a plane?

No. It's Superman!

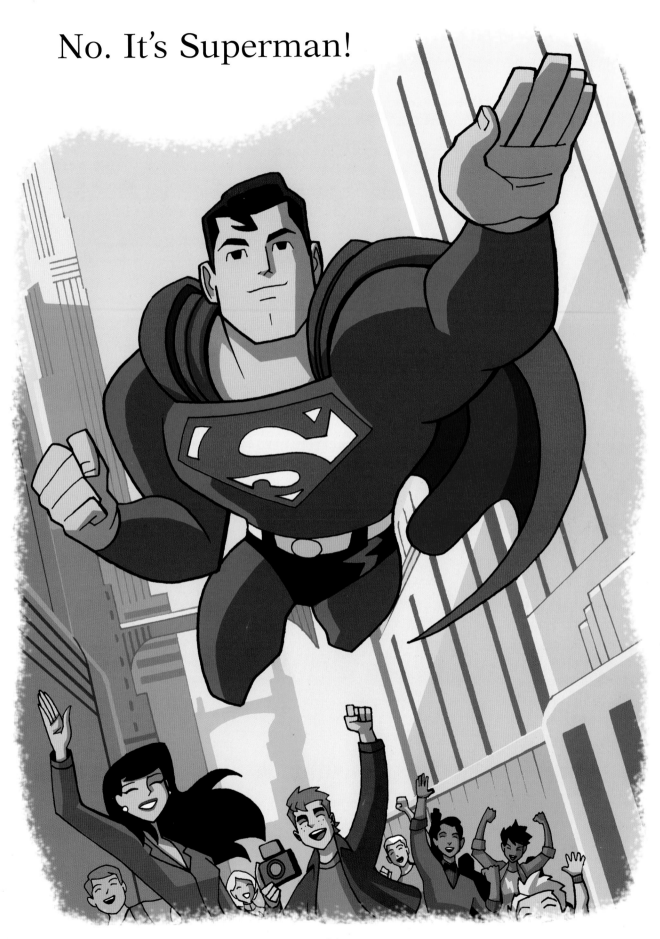

SUPERMAN ™

EARTH NAME: CLARK KENT

REAL NAME: KAL-EL

ROLE: PROTECTOR OF EARTH

BASE: METROPOLIS

Clark Kent is a mild-mannered reporter. The Man of Steel is the super-powered protector of Earth. Although quite different on the outside, these two men are secretly the same person!

The Man of Steel can use heat vision to melt solid objects.

His X-ray vision can see through anything but lead.

The S-Shield is Superman's symbol.

Superman's breath can blow away criminals or cool off burning objects.

Up, up and away! Superman can fly through the sky!

Superman is invulnerable, meaning he cannot be harmed unless weakened by Kryptonite.

Superman has super-strength and super-speed.

THE AUTHOR

Over the course of **MATTHEW K. MANNING**'s writing career, he has written comics or books starring Batman, Superman, the Flash, the Justice League and even Bugs Bunny. Some of his more recent works include *The Batman Files*, a graphic novel retelling of *The Fall of the House of Usher* and several DC Super Heroes books. He lives in Connecticut, USA, with his wife Dorothy and daughter Lillian.

THE ILLUSTRATOR

LUCIANO VECCHIO has experience in illustration, animation and comics, and his works have been published in the UK, USA, Spain, France and Argentina. His credits include Ben 10 (DC Comics), Cruel Thing (Norma), Unseen Tribe (Zuda Comics) and Sentinels (Drumfish Productions). He lives in Buenos Aires, Argentina.

 GLOSSARY

assignment task or piece of work given to someone

conductor person who collects tickets from passengers on a train

device object, machine or piece of equipment made for some special purpose

fateful if something is fateful, it will be very important later on

invulnerable unable to be harmed or damaged

malfunction fail to work properly

realize understand or become aware of something

recite read something out loud or say something from memory (usually for an audience)

reveal show something plainly or clearly, often for the first time

universe all of space and everything in it including stars, planets and galaxies

DISCUSSION QUESTIONS

Write down your answers. Refer back to the story for help.

QUESTION 1.

This illustration of Clark is on page 15. Based on how he looks in this shot, how do you think Clark feels? Why do you think he feels this way?

QUESTION 2.

On page 19, Jonathan and Martha Kent give Clark this device. Based on what happens next in the story, what do you think this device is? What does it do?

QUESTION 3.

Who do you think this red-headed young man is? Why is he taking photos of Superman?

QUESTION 4.

What clue did the illustrator give readers about who is inside the ship in this illustration?

Hint: it involves the rocket's path of travel.

READ THEM ALL!!

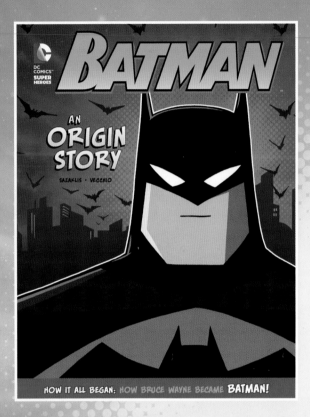

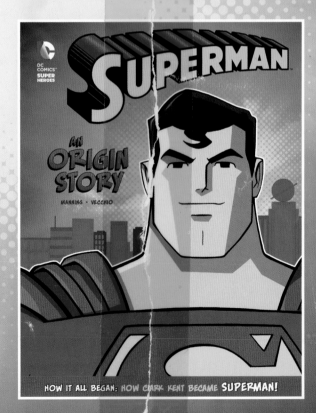